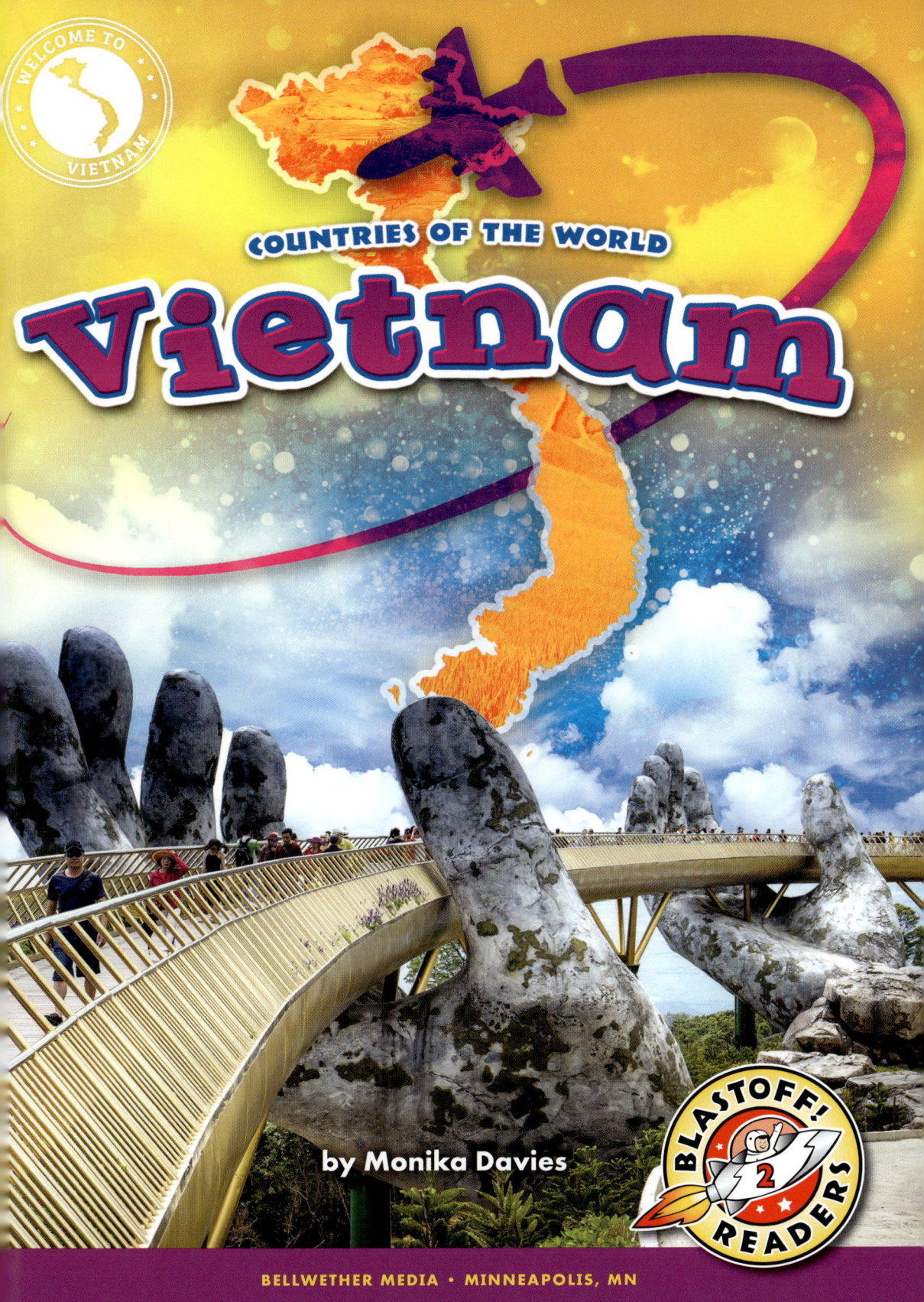

Blastoff! Readers are carefully developed by literacy experts to build reading stamina and move students toward fluency by combining standards-based content with developmentally appropriate text.

Level 1 provides the most support through repetition of high-frequency words, light text, predictable sentence patterns, and strong visual support.

Level 2 offers early readers a bit more challenge through varied sentences, increased text load, and text-supportive special features.

Level 3 advances early-fluent readers toward fluency through increased text load, less reliance on photos, advancing concepts, longer sentences, and more complex special features.

★ **Blastoff! Universe**

Reading Level

 Grade K

 Grades 1–3

 Grade 4

This edition first published in 2023 by Bellwether Media, Inc.

No part of this publication may be reproduced in whole or in part without written permission of the publisher. For information regarding permission, write to Bellwether Media, Inc., Attention: Permissions Department, 6012 Blue Circle Drive, Minnetonka, MN 55343.

Library of Congress Cataloging-in-Publication Data

LC record for Vietnam available at: https://lccn.loc.gov/2022044141

Text copyright © 2023 by Bellwether Media, Inc. BLASTOFF! READERS and associated logos are trademarks and/or registered trademarks of Bellwether Media, Inc.

Editor: Elizabeth Neuenfeldt   Designer: Gabriel Hilger

Printed in the United States of America, North Mankato, MN.

Table of Contents

All About Vietnam	4
Land and Animals	6
Life in Vietnam	12
Vietnam Facts	20
Glossary	22
To Learn More	23
Index	24

All About Vietnam

Hanoi

Vietnam is in Southeast Asia. It lies along the South China Sea. Its capital is Hanoi.

Vietnam is a growing nation. More than 103 million people call it home!

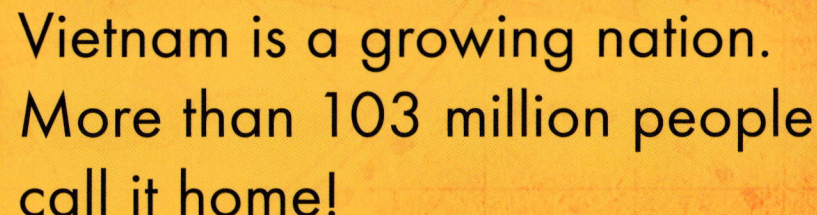

Land and Animals

Mountains cover much of Vietnam. Lowlands lie to the south.

The Red River flows in the north. The Mekong River flows in the south. They form **deltas** on the east coast.

Mekong River

Size: about 2,700 miles (4,345 kilometers) long

Famous For: longest river in Southeast Asia

Vietnam is mostly hot and **humid**. It rains a lot, too!

Monsoons control the country's **climate**. These winds change direction every season.

monsoon

Vietnam is full of wildlife! Black bears live in forests. Snub-nosed monkeys swing between trees in the mountains.

Asiatic black bear

Animals of Vietnam

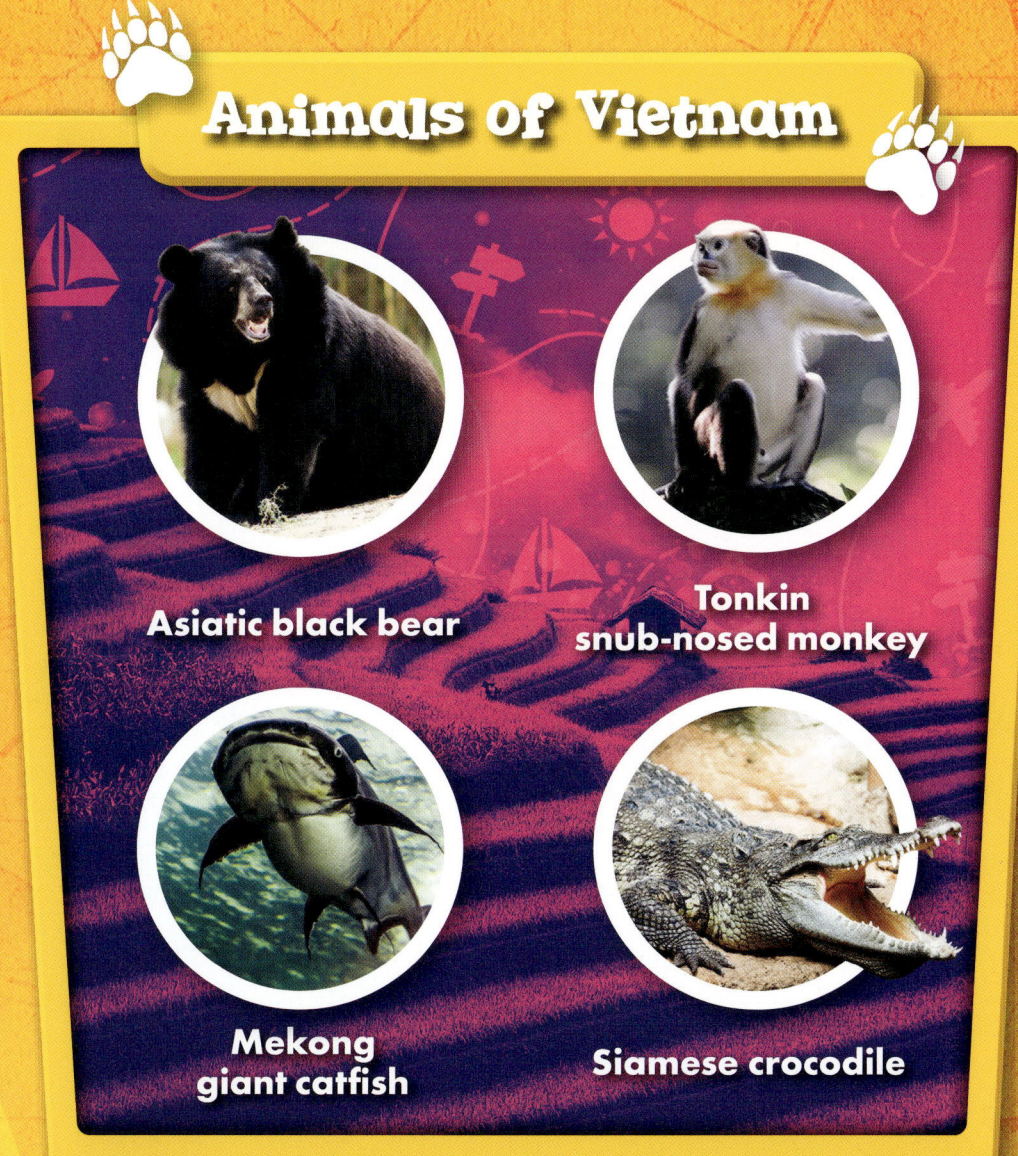

Asiatic black bear

Tonkin snub-nosed monkey

Mekong giant catfish

Siamese crocodile

Mekong giant catfish swim in rivers. Crocodiles hunt nearby.

Life in Vietnam

More than 100 languages are spoken in Vietnam! Most people speak Vietnamese.

Many Vietnamese people work as farmers. Most live near the river deltas.

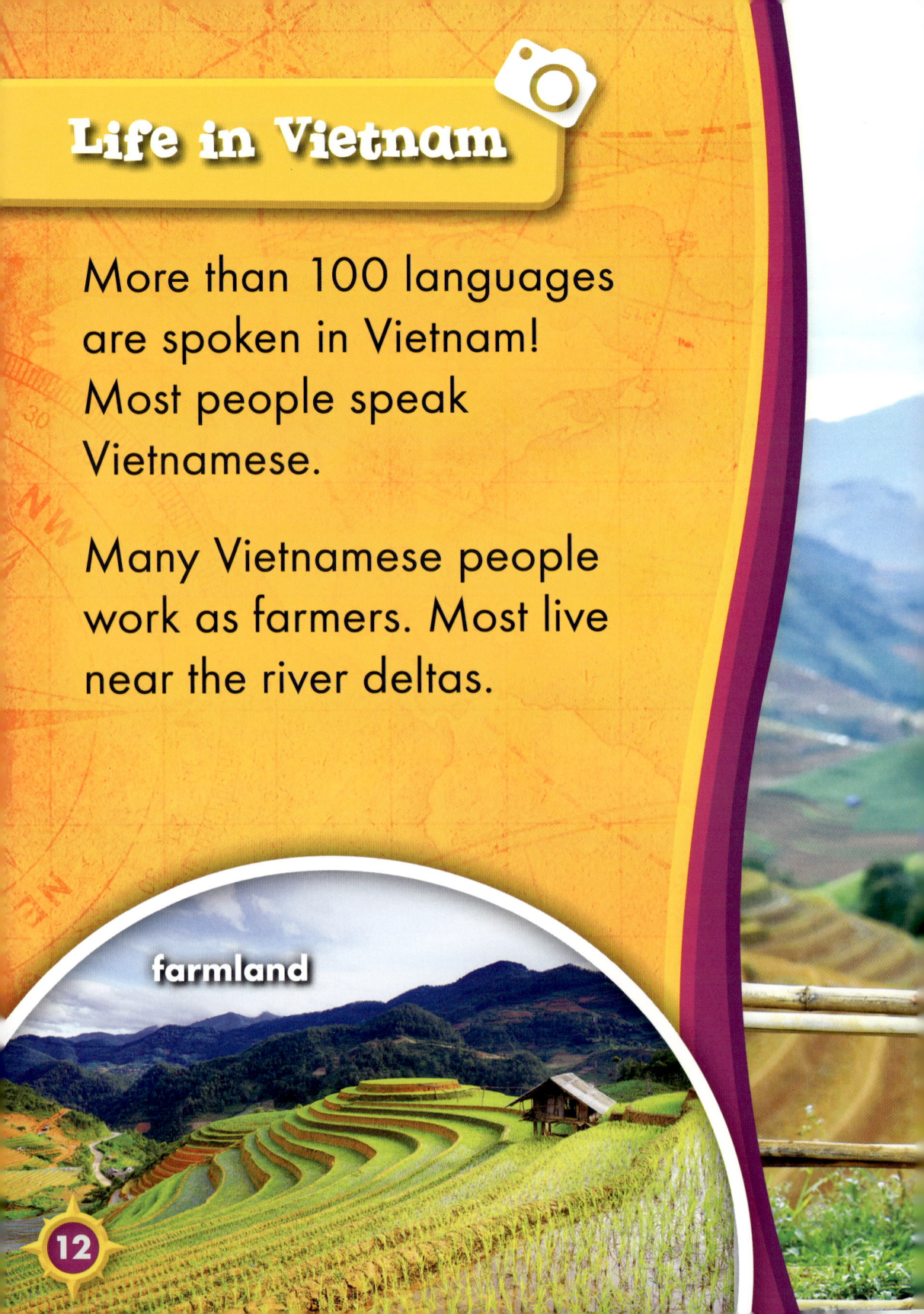

farmland

soccer

volleyball

Soccer is a top sport in Vietnam. Volleyball is also popular.

Many Vietnamese people practice *vovinam* or *tai chi*. They are types of **martial arts**.

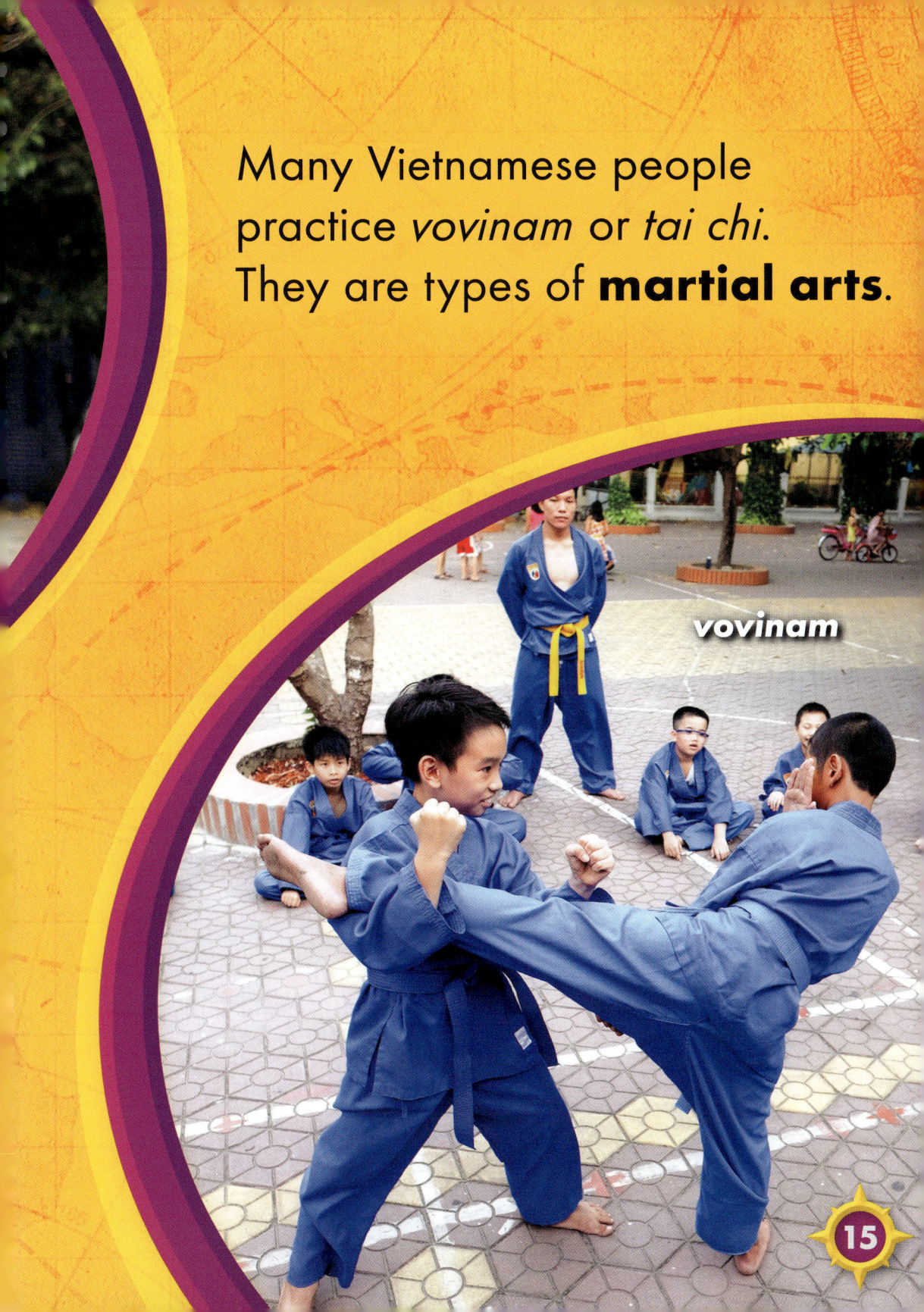

vovinam

Rice is a **staple** food in Vietnam. *Pho* is a noodle soup. *Gói cuôn* is a fresh spring roll.

Vietnamese Foods

rice

pho

gói cuôn

xi mà

Xi mà is a popular dessert. It is black sesame soup!

Tết

Tết marks the **lunar** new year. Families give gifts and share big meals.

September 2 is Vietnam's national holiday. People fly flags and watch parades. Holidays bring Vietnamese people together!

Vietnam Facts

Size:
127,881 square miles
(331,210 square kilometers)

Population:
103,808,319 (2022)

National Holiday:
Independence Day (September 2)

Main Language:
Vietnamese

Capital City:
Hanoi

Famous Face

Name: Xuân Vinh Hoàng

Famous For: a sport shooter who became the first Olympic gold medalist in Vietnam's history

Religions

- none 86%
- Catholic 6%
- other 2%
- Buddhist 6%

Top Landmarks

Ha Long Bay

Imperial City of Hué

Temple of Literature

Glossary

climate—the usual weather conditions in a certain place

deltas—pieces of land shaped like triangles that are formed when rivers split into smaller rivers before they empty into oceans

humid—having a lot of water in the air

lunar—related to the moon

martial arts—different sports or skills that first started as ways to fight or stay safe

monsoons—winds that shift direction each season; monsoons bring heavy rain.

staple—a widely used food or other item

To Learn More

AT THE LIBRARY

Grack, Rachel. *Crocodiles*. Minneapolis, Minn.: Bellwether Media, 2020.

Phi, Bao. *A Different Pond*. North Mankato, Minn.: Picture Window Books, 2017.

Spanier, Kristine. *Vietnam*. Minneapolis, Minn.: Jump! Inc., 2020.

ON THE WEB

FACTSURFER

Factsurfer.com gives you a safe, fun way to find more information.

1. Go to www.factsurfer.com.
2. Enter "Vietnam" into the search box and click 🔍.
3. Select your book cover to see a list of related content.

Index

animals, 10, 11
Asia, 4
capital (see Hanoi)
deltas, 6, 12
food, 16, 17
Hanoi, 4, 5
map, 5
martial arts, 15
Mekong River, 6, 7
monsoons, 9
mountains, 6, 10
national holiday, 19
people, 5, 12, 15, 19
rain, 8
Red River, 6
say hello, 13

soccer, 14
South China Sea, 4
Tết, 18
Vietnam facts, 20–21
Vietnamese, 12, 13
volleyball, 14

The images in this book are reproduced through the courtesy of: Quang nguyen vinh, cover, pp. 8-9; Jeroen Mikkers, cover; pudiq, p. 3; Le Thanh Hoang Vu, pp. 4-5, 15; Maksim Semin, p. 6; incamerastock/ Alamy, pp. 6-7; pcruciatti, p. 9; Volodymyr Burdiak, pp. 10-11; OSTILL, p. 11 (Asiatic black bear); Quyet Le/ Wikipedia, p. 11 (Tonkin snub-nosed monkey); Thussapon.28, p. 11 (Mekong giant catfish); BearFotos, p. 11 (Siamese crocodile); naihei, p. 12; jiraphoto, pp. 12-13; CatwalkPhotos, pp. 14-15; daykung, p. 14 (inset); WIROJE PATHI, p. 16 (rice); Anna_Pustynnikova, p. 16 (*pho*); xuanhuongho, p. 16 (*Gỏi cuốn*); TravelTelly, p. 16 (*xì mà*); p. 17 hadynyah, p. 17; vinhdav, pp. 18-19; titoOnz, p. 20 (flag); Sam Greenwood/ Staff/ Getty Images, p. 20 (Hoàng Xuân Vinh); PhotoRoman, p. 21 (Ha Long Bay); Chris Cozz, p. 21 (Imperial City of Hué); Traveller. P, p. 21 (Temple of Literature); konmesa, pp. 22-23.